Buffy's Re

Library of Congress cataloging-in-publication data

Sargent, David M.,   1966-
  Buffy's revenge / by David M. Sargent, Jr. ; illustrated by Jean Lirley Huff.
    p. cm.
  Summary: Two dachshunds are jealous of a fluffy pomeranian, so they attack her and
rip out her fur, but the pomeranian's revenge proves sweet.
  ISBN 1-56763-332-3 (CB : alk. paper). -- ISBN 1-56763-333-1 (PB : alk. paper)
  [1. Dogs--Fiction.   2. Revenger--Fiction.   3. Stories in rhyme.]
  I. Huff, Jean Jean , 1946-   ill. II. Title
  PZ8.3.S2355Bu   1997
  [E]--dc21

                       96-54583
                       CIP
                         AC

Buffy's Revenge

By

David M. Sargent, Jr.

Illustrated by

Jean Lirley Huff

Ozark Publishing, Inc.
P.O. Box 228
Prairie Grove, AR 72753

Vera Bardot was the most beautiful girl,
Whose jet black hair had not one curl.

She liked to run and she liked to play.
Inside the house, she'd never stay.

Chasing the ball was her favorite sport.
When picking it up, she'd often snort.

Her very best friend was known as Buff,
A darling pom with lots of white fluff.

Buffy was prettier than Vera, it's true.
So, Vera had a thought. She knew what to do.

She yanked and she pulled. She tugged and she laughed.
Soon Buff's hair was gone. She looked quite sad.

Buffy just smiled and went on her way.
She had decided just how she'd repay.

As time went by, Vera grew wary.
She could only wonder about Buffy's fury.

Oh, and yes, I forgot to mention
Little Miss Mary and her bad disposition.

She laughed and she teased Buff of her lost hair.
She was just plain mean and didn't seem to care.

Again, Buffy just smiled and went on her way,
For she knew revenge was hers someday.

Mary and Vera prayed as they went to bed,
For the fear of Buffy's fury filled them with
dread.

Buffy's revenge . . . some say was so sweet.
With Mary and Vera she shared her daily treat.

She killed them with kindness and for this they were sore.
Eventually, her hair grew back more beautiful than ever before.